UNWITTING WISDOM

To Aesop
and all tellers of moral tales who,
despite a monumentally ineffective history,
still gently try to point the human race
in a better direction - h.w.

ଏ A TEMPLAR BOOK ଓ

This edition published in 2004 by Templar Publishing,
an imprint of The Templar Company plc,
Pippbrook Mill, London Road, Dorking, Surrey, RH4 1JE, UK
www.templarco.co.uk

FIRST EDITION

ISBN 1-84011-429-0

Edited by A. J. Wood
Typography by Mike Jolley

The illustrations in this book are rendered in ink line and watercolour
on cotton-rag watercolour paper
The text is set in Leonardo & MB Tempus

Printed in Hong Kong

Unwitting WISDOM

An anthology of Aesop's animal fables

RETOLD & ILLUSTRATED BY

HELEN WARD

templar publishing

Aesop's Fables

helen ward

AESOP'S FABLES

REMAIN AMONG THE MOST ENDURING OF STORIES.

The seeming simplicity of such tales as "The Lion and the Mouse" and "The Hare and the Tortoise" belie the strength of their underlying message, and the final moral once heard is seldom forgotten. But Aesop himself remains something of a mystery. Some say that he was a Greek slave who lived in the late 5th century B.C. and made up the original tales to amuse his master, others that Aesop is a collective name under which the best and earliest fables have been gathered and passed down through generations. Whatever their true origin, variations of these stories appear the world over, particularly in Ancient Greece, Egypt and India.

IN THIS EDITION award-winning illustrator Helen Ward has collected together a dozen of her favourites, including fables both familiar and lesser-known. All use animals as the central characters in place of people, thereby avoiding the distractions of race or class, age or gender. As such, the experiences described apply to us all and the lessons learned are both timeless and universal. Each creature comes to symbolize in its own way some particular aspect of the human condition — the sly, sidling fox; the silly crow; the majestic lion; all acting out their parts, uncomprehending, in the great game of life. As the author G.K. Chesterton once wrote, "In Aesop's Fables... the animals' reactions are always predictable. They have no choice; they cannot be anything but themselves. They are never more or less, and that is the great lesson and the essence of the fable."

Here then is a panoply of human feeling expressed through Ward's animals. Fear, greed, arrogance, stupidity, all these and more put in an appearance, leaping straight to the heart of our understanding from each page of this magnificent edition.

sour grapes

IN
WHICH
A
FOX
TRIES
TO
HIDE
HIS
DISAPPOINTMENT
WITH
INSULTS

THERE WAS ONCE A BUNCH OF PARTICULARLY FINE GRAPES

hanging temptingly from a vine that had wound its way up a tree. And as is usual with such unguarded temptations THERE WAS SOON ALSO A FOX.

The tantalising fruits hung just a little higher than the fox could reach but he would not be thwarted.

He leapt as high as he could, twisting in the morning light, his jaws clapping shut on air and flies and dust until his teeth hurt. He tried to climb the tree but the trunk was too straight, the bark too smooth, the first branch too high. Everything about the tree was unhelpful. It refused to so much as twitch a twig when he tried to shake it.

The fox found a long cane and tried to prod the grapes from their vine, but the cane snapped. He threw and kicked sticks and stones at the vine, but the grapes were determined to stay put. Their sweet smell drifted among the branches, wasps and butterflies flew by with casual ease, while on the ground below the fox lay panting and exhausted. Not even a few minutes' patience solved the fox's problem. By the evening the dark fruits hung as resolutely from the vine as they had that morning.

The shadows had lengthened by the time the fox finally turned his back on the grapes, muttering to himself that they were undoubtedly

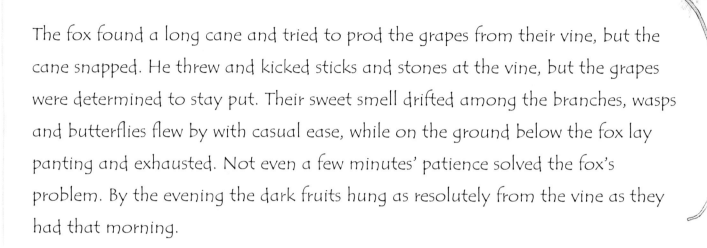

THE NASTIEST, MOST HORRID, DISGUSTING, REVOLTING, INEDIBLE, INDIGESTIBLE and very probably the SOUREST grapes he had ever had the pleasure of NOT eating!

଼ IT IS EASY TO DESPISE WHAT YOU CANNOT OBTAIN ଼

the trappings of power

IN WHICH

THE POWERFUL

PERISH THROUGH

THEIR PRIDE

THERE ONCE WAS A CITY OF MICE, fortified

against marauders with high, thick walls, perforated only by a hundred little exits or entrances just big enough for a mouse and just small enough to keep out anything larger and more dangerous… IN PARTICULAR, WEASELS.

The mice and the weasels had been at war for longer than anyone could remember. So long that neither the mice nor the weasels knew why. All they knew was that they hated each other, and that was enough to fight battle after battle. But this long war had cost the mice dear, for in all the time they had been fighting they had lost every battle and many a mouse to their ferocious enemy.

At long last the mice decided to have a conference. They concluded that their problem was a lack of discipline on the battlefield. No attack had ever been co-ordinated, no retreat anything other than every-mouse-for-himself. They decided that what they needed was organisation and leadership.

So they chose from among themselves some leaders. Charismatic mice who promised victory on the battlefield, mice whose very first act as generals was to order themselves some particularly shiny swords and the very grandest and most exclusive battle helmets with wide, imposing horns. Then, after a very good meal, they sat idly picking their gleaming teeth and passing the port.

The next day the mouse army assembled on the battlefield, with new hope and keenness, to await the advance of the weasels, but when the onslaught came the mice were no more organised than before. As usual the army scattered and fled for the safety of the city. They scuttled through their mouse holes, all except the new generals who were a little too sluggish on their feet and, with the glamorous horns on their gleaming helmets too wide to slip easily through, they were simply captured by the enemy and taken away.

all dressed up

IN WHICH A JACKDAW
"BORROWS"
SOME FEATHERS

THERE WAS ONCE A JACKDAW

who was as black as soot with a bright eye, a voice like a broken bell and some NASTY HABITS that she couldn't help.

She wanted to be a popular and important bird, so she was very careful to be ever so polite and ever so attentive to any bird who had already achieved such status; to cackle loud and long at their bad jokes and compliment their looks, however dull, far, far too often. She was inclined to tread on the sparrows on her way to see the influential eagles and was surprised to find at the end of all her efforts that she was still a very ordinary jackdaw.

One day the jackdaw heard that there was to be a competition to find the most beautiful bird, and she determined that she must win it. Despite being rather plain she had an idea or two behind that glinting eye...

She followed the brighter birds around and collected the feathers that they dropped so carelessly about the place. The sparrows were intrigued but kept their distance, not wanting to lose their own feathers to such an avid collector.

Each evening in her roost the jackdaw cleaned and combed her growing collection. She sorted them by size and colour and threw out those that were too dull or beyond repair. The night before the competition the jackdaw carefully slotted the abandoned feathers in amongst her own. With their stripes and spots, blotches and patches, she settled each in place to create a riotous rainbow of colour, as neat and perfect as if it had grown there of its own accord. She looked quite beautiful in her borrowed feathers. Now it was her turn to shine.

The competitors ruffled up their gorgeous plumes and puffed out their chests. They strutted about and the jackdaw strutted among them, prouder than a peacock, stealing the attention of the judges with a swish of her purloined tail. Who in the audience could resist this sparkling, effervescent bird?

There was no doubt about the winner. THE JACKDAW WAS CERTAINLY THE MOST BEAUTIFUL.

Suddenly, a kerfuffle broke out in the audience. It spread through the crowds and among the competitors. They each began to recognise something familiar in the pattern and the colour of this glamorous bird. They snatched and plucked their feathers back until the deceitful jackdaw was revealed, quite undressed and plain and dull and rather dishevelled. Without her borrowed finery, with no prize for being the most beautiful, no audience to please, no important friends and nothing remarkable to be or to say, she had only herself for company and some hard thinking to be done.

ℰↃ FINE FEATHERS ℂℛ
DO NOT MAKE FINE BIRDS

pot luck

IN WHICH A
WOLF'S CUNNING IS
HIS OWN
DOWNFALL

THERE WAS ONCE A WOLF

WHO WAS UNHAPPY WITH HIS LOT IN LIFE.

He thought, among other things, that he was very clever and that too much of his valuable time was spent running about risking life and limb just to fill his belly. And when his belly was full he had to spend the rest of his day moping about in a dingy hole or lurking in the shadows. So he applied his agile and cunning mind to considering how his life might be made easier.

He needed to live closer to his supper, and his most favourite supper was sheep. He needed camouflage. He could be a hedge, or a rock… or something altogether more devious.

As fortune would have it, the very next day the wolf found the remains of a dead ewe and, having wrapped himself carefully in her skin, he joined a flock of her woolly-brained sisters, quite unnoticed.

Standing in the warm morning sun, he listened to their inane gossip. In the
afternoon he lounged about among the flowers and butterflies. He learned all
he didn't need to know about grass. While the crickets churred and the shadows
grew long, he lazily cast an eye over his meadow-munching meal.

In the evening he moved with the contented, murmuring flock to the close
comfort of the sheepfold. The wolf's attention turned to his grumbling stomach,
and his head filled with the self-satisfied thoughts of one whose plans were working
so well, whose easy future now stretched ahead into a thousand dreamy rose-
coloured sunsets, but whose fat, woolly back had caught the eye of the shepherd.

His grumbling stomach was also matched by a head filled with thoughts…
of roasted mutton.

The wolf's disguise was SO VERY CLEVER,
SO VERY EFFECTIVE,
SO VERY, VERY LIKE A SHEEP
that it lasted right through to the last tender,

tasty

morsel.

 ❧ HARM SEEK, HARM FIND ☙

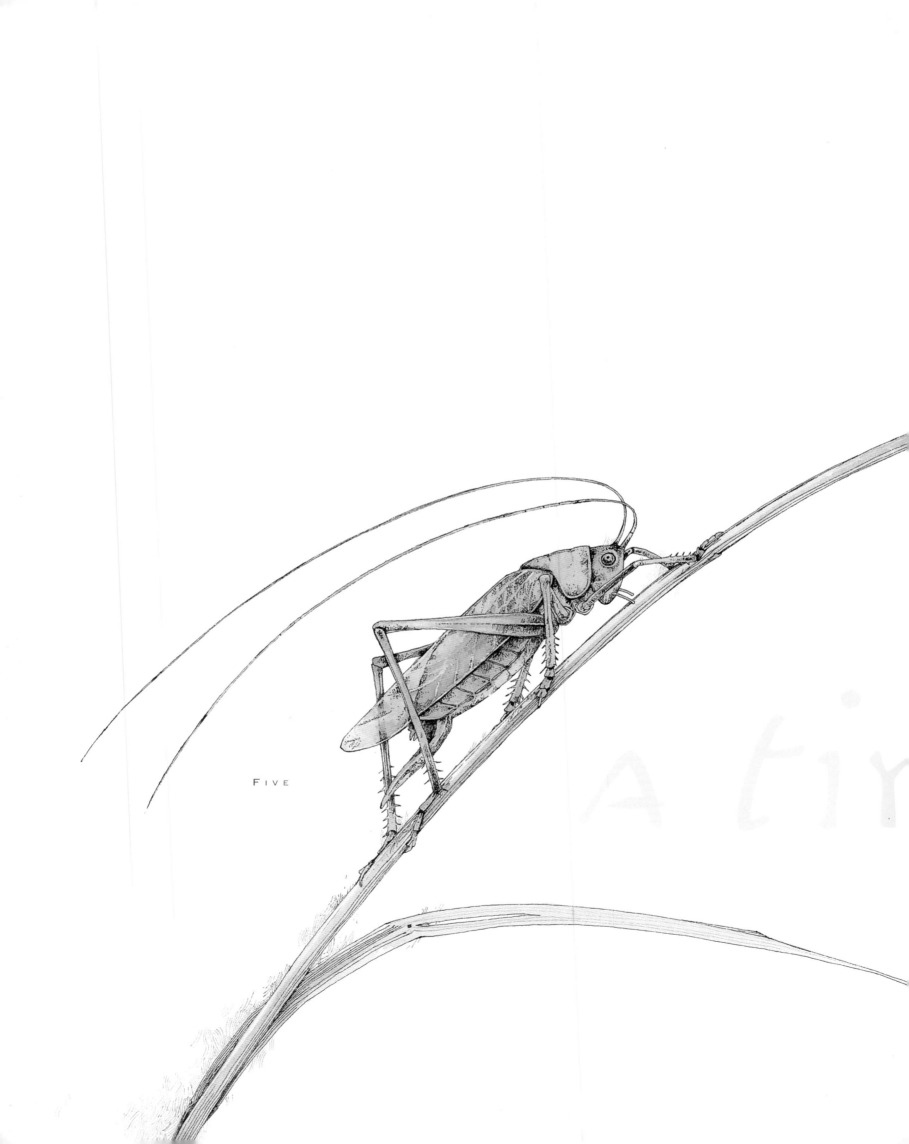

FIVE

...he industrious ants were everywhere, busy in the warm weather: occupied in the season of plenty, with ceaseless searching among the grasses where a cricket sang, in the meadows. Like

...e to dance

IN WHICH A CRICKET LEARNS ABOUT WORK —

THE HARD WAY

THERE WAS ONCE A CRICKET,

A VERY HAPPY CREATURE WITH NOT A CARE IN THE WORLD and not an idea in his head. He had never been burdened by great thoughts or bothered by the smaller, more useful ones that slipped from his head like down from a thistle. As long as the sun shone each day he was content to sit on a barley stalk and sing.

He ate when he was hungry, he slept when he was tired, and since the sun shone all summer, all summer he sang.

In autumn the cold began to bite. Food became surprisingly scarce, so the cricket grew hollow with hunger. He no longer felt inclined to sing, but shivered and rattled instead. It was well known that the ANTS had plentiful supplies, but nobody had dared to try their generosity. Nevertheless, the cricket left his barley stalk and set off for the ants' fortress...

traffic on a fast road, noisily they ticked across the dried leaves, an army of small footfalls, up and down gnarled tree trunks to their aphid herds, hau

The cricket begged one of the guards for a little something to eat.

"How can you be hungry?" demanded the ant. "Winter is only just starting.

What have you done with your stores of food?"

"Stores?" said the cricket.

"Food put away to eat in the winter. Stores of food from the months when there

was plenty. What," asked the ant (though no more kindly), "have you been

doing all summer?!"

"I was busy...," whined the cricket (and he had to admit it sounded a little silly

on a frosty morning), "...singing."

The ant of course was unimpressed. "Then MAYBE...," he said acidly,

"...YOU SHOULD DANCE ALL WINTER." And with that, he turned

his back on the cricket and marched into the nest.

&ent; Do Not Put Off Until Tomorrow &ent;
What You Should Do Today

SIX

A dinner in

IN WHICH A FOX IS A BAD HOST AND A HUNGRY GUEST

THERE WAS ONCE A STORK,

A TALL AND ELEGANT BIRD, very polite and refined in her habits. She moved to a new neighbourhood and fairly soon received an invitation to dinner. It was from one of the local residents, A FOX.

She knew nothing of the nature of foxes, so when she arrived for dinner she was only a little taken aback to find every course served in shallow dishes. Showing no consideration for his guest the fox lapped his way through the delicious meal with an all too apparent gusto. The stork could only dip the very tip of her beak into the various sauces. She went home more than a little hungry, not to mention offended, while the fox happily finished off the leftovers.

Some weeks later the stork, being a well brought up bird, sent a dinner invitation to the fox. The fox was only too pleased to accept. He liked nothing better than a good meal at someone else's expense.

He did not know that the stork would repay him with a taste of the same consideration that he had shown his own guest.

The stork invited the fox into the dining room. He was tantalised by the wonderful smells wafting through the room. His mouth watered at the prospect of a sumptuous feast, but there was no platter of roasted meats, no dish of gravy or bowl of sauce in the room. Not one morsel of the delicious-smelling food was served in anything other than tall, narrow-mouthed jars, all perfect for the

LONG
BEAK
OF A
STORK.

Each elegant vessel, fragrant with the promise of food, stopped the fox's snout aggravatingly short of his reach. The stork appeared oblivious to his dilemma. Despite the grandness of the occasion and the polite attentions of the stork, not so much as a buttered pea passed his lips all evening.

The fox went home very hungry and very perplexed. It took him quite a while to work out why he had deserved such treatment. When he finally understood, he felt no better, for he was not at all used to being outsmarted.

ℂ Do As You Would Be Done By ℂ

SEVEN

steady and slow

IN WHICH A HARE IS TOO
CONFIDENT

THERE WAS ONCE A VERY FAST HARE

AND A VERY SLOW TORTOISE. The hare liked nothing better than impressing the general population with his speed. "I am the master of being faster," was how he so irritatingly put it.

The general population, on the other hand, liked nothing better than discussing the small size of the hare's brain, and where he kept it while he was hurtling about, and how long it would take a crocodile to eat him if he accidentally ran into the river, and whether or not anyone would try to rescue him. Most admitted to a profound respect for the crocodile's teeth but none for any part of the hare.

The tortoise suffered from the hare more than most. The hare humiliated him at every opportunity, but the tortoise was just too gentle and too slow to retaliate.

Before he could say or do anything, the hare was long gone. So the tortoise decided to challenge the hare to a race. The general population thought this was unusually stupid of the tortoise. The hare thought only how certain he was to win. But the tortoise knew what he was doing, the hare being so very predictable.

The race began and the hare hurtled off into the distance. The tortoise plodded forward, settling his thoughts on higher things. Even when the hare hurtled back and ran a few rings around him, the tortoise felt no need to change his even, patient pace.

With so little to challenge his supremacy, the hare decided to take a short nap. The nap turned into a bit of a doze, the doze into a long snooze... until the hare fell fast into a proper sleep. Meanwhile the tortoise plodded steadily on until he passed the deep-dreaming hare. None of the general population had disturbed him. The tortoise was almost at the finishing post when the hare woke up and shook his thoughts into some sort of order. He remembered he was supposed to be winning something. A RACE?

BUT IT WAS TOO LATE...

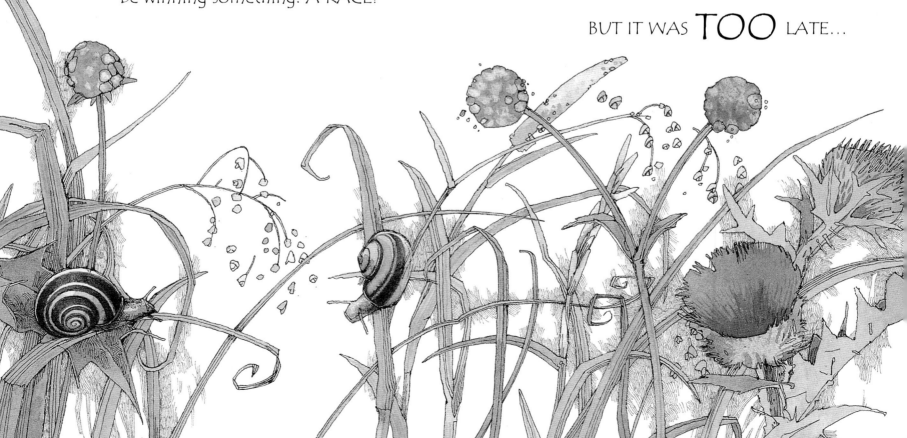

...As the hare came speeding up to the finishing post THE TORTOISE
CROSSED THE LINE AND WON.

The hare was thoroughly humiliated. For a long time afterwards the general
population made snoring noises whenever the hare was in earshot or glanced
into the distance to shout "TORTOISE COMING!" None of this did much to slow
the hare down, but he was at least less annoying, and there was still a good
chance that someday he would end up testing the hardness of a tree trunk, or the
firmness of the ground at the end of a long drop or, of course, the sharpness of
a crocodile's teeth...

꽃 SLOW AND STEADY 꽃
WINS THE RACE

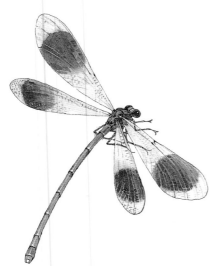

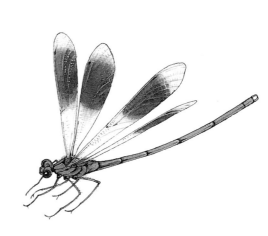

IN WHICH

HE WHO WOULD HAVE EVERYTHING,

GETS NOTHING

THERE WAS ONCE A DOG

WHO, one way or another,
TOOK THE VERY BEST OF EVERYTHING.

He was not a "fetch" or a "sit" or a "stay" kind of dog. He was a nose-led "do my own thing", "go my own way" kind of dog to whom every unguarded tabletop, bowl, bin, kitchen or butcher's shop belonged. One day he stole a particularly fine bone, right off of a recklessly unguarded butcher's counter, and made off with it up the street. It was so large that he could barely run with it, but run he did leaving the angry shopkeeper behind with only his shaking fist for company.

The dog trotted homeward proudly, gripping his prize firmly between his teeth, so that anyone passing might admire it. With a spring in his step and his tail in the air, he had no other thought in his head than the satisfying certainty that he owned the very best of all bones and that was just how things should be.

He headed for home and a private corner where he could enjoy his prize or bury it unseen so as to savour the moment awhile.

His chosen path took him over a bridge across a pool in a calm river. No sooner had the dog stepped onto the first plank than something caught his eye. Another dog looking far too pleased with himself was staring at him from among the lily pads. Worse, this dog too had a bone, and how much larger and juicier it looked than his own.

Being among other things a greedy, jealous, thieving kind of creature, the dog on the bridge did not hesitate. Without thinking further, he lunged forward with snapping jaws, dropping his own bone as he tried to snatch the larger one.

SPLASH! As soon as his muzzle hit the water, the second dog disappeared and his jaws snapped hard shut on nothing. His reflection, for that indeed is all it had been, broke and splintered into shimmering ripples, spreading out across the pool until all was still again.

When the greedy dog looked down he could see that it was his own image that had fooled him. And worse, that solid nonillusion of a bone that he had so recently released from the butcher's custody, that wholesome promise of genuine pleasure, had fallen from his mouth and was gone. For one tiny moment it had been overlooked in favour of something more magnificent, something that turned out to be as insubstantial as a dream. Now it was lost, dropped into the river, as much a memory as its reflection. The only thing left on the dog's mind was the fact of his own stupidity, and he slunk home with a low tail and a hollow stomach.

BE GRATEFUL FOR WHAT YOU HAVE

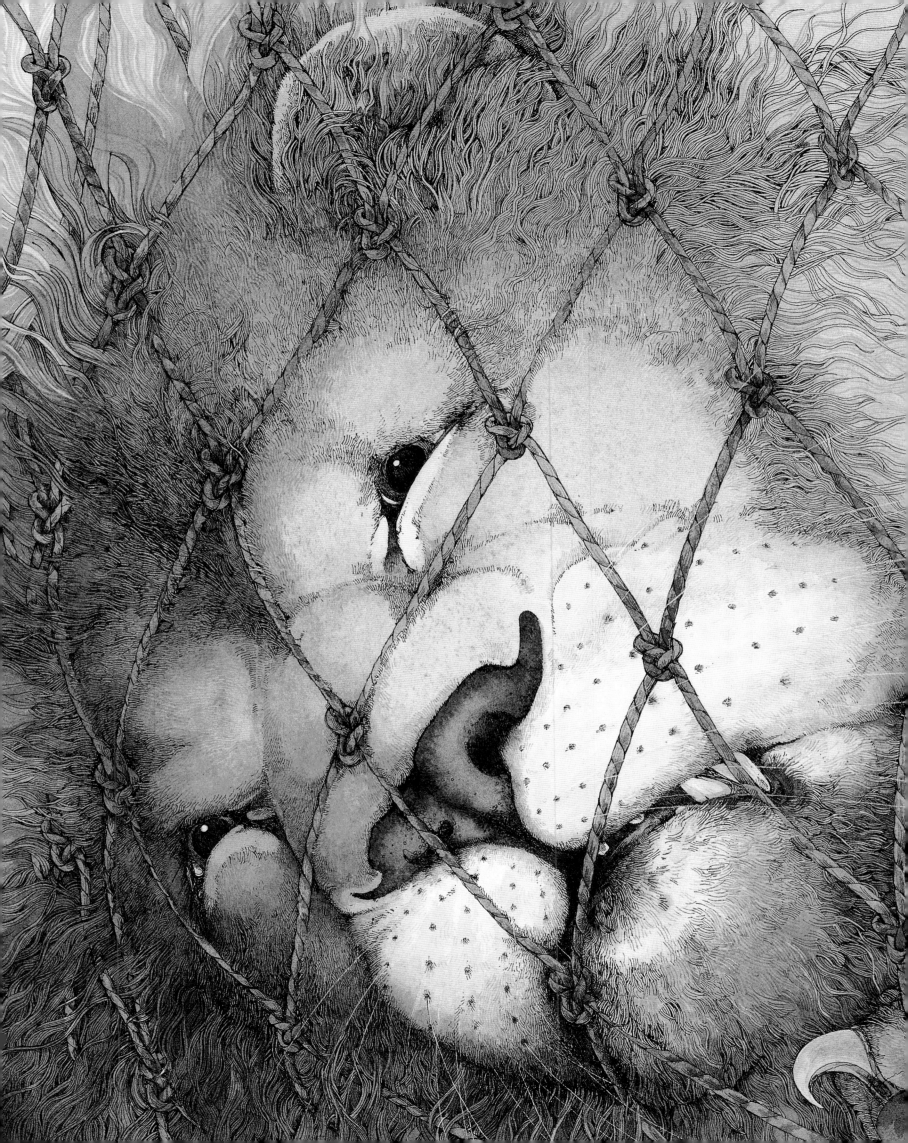

size isn't everything

NINE

IN WHICH A MOUSE UNEXPECTEDLY
RETURNS A FAVOUR

THERE
WAS ONCE
A LION

sleeping peacefully in the shade of a cedar tree when
A MOUSE mistook him for a boulder and scrambled across his
shoulders. The lion woke and shuddered like an earthquake
under the little creature, shaking him to the ground where he
caught the mouse by the tail beneath one great paw.

The mouse was terrified. The lion eyed the smallness of the
soon-to-be-eaten sight before him and sniffed the mousiness
of this less-than-a-mouthful squeaker. The mouse trembled.
Almost too scared to say anything, he begged to be set free.

The lion yawned absentmindedly, revealing his cavernous,
tooth-ringed mouth, his coarse pink tongue and the dark threat
of his throat. He breathed upon the mouse the very breath
of doom.

The mouse squeaked again. "Please let me go and I give you my
word that one day I will return the favour."

"You give your word, squeaking pip?" asked the lion, laughing at the mouse's impertinence. The mouse nodded as well as he could, and the lion lifted his great paw and let the little creature free. They went their separate ways. The lion thought nothing more of the mouse, but the mouse was far more careful of where he put his feet.

Then one day the roar of the lion rang pitifully through the forest. It woke the mouse in the close comfort of his nest. There was sadness in the echoing roar and, as it shook the pine needles from the trees, the mouse hurried towards it, mindful of the promise he had made. The lion, huge and fierce though he was, now hung from a great branch, caught in a hunter's net and trapped so tightly in its entangling mesh that he could not move. The mouse quickly climbed up the tree and down the thick ropes where he set to work with his sharp white teeth. He chewed and pulled and frayed and nibbled and gnawed through the mesh until eventually the net began to loosen. Limb by limb, the lion was released, falling ungainly as a newborn calf onto the forest floor.

The lion tried to look as humble as he felt, thanking the mouse profusely and promising never to underestimate the smaller creatures again. The mouse in turn tried to look heroic and brave and as unlike a tasty snack as he could. It was with some relief and not a little pride that he watched as the lion disappeared into the shadows of the forest.

℘ IT HOLDS THROUGH THE WHOLE ℘
SCALE OF CREATION THAT THE GREAT AND THE SMALL
HAVE NEED, ONE OF THE OTHER

IN WHICH A TORTOISE IGNORES EXPERT ADVICE

not flying, but falling

THERE WAS ONCE A TORTOISE

whose head was always in the clouds, though the rest of him all too firmly hugged the earth. THE TORTOISE DREAMED, as no other tortoise had dreamed, OF FLYING.

Swallows scooted low across the grassland, rich blue darts of squealing, aggravating speed, each flit and turn filling the tortoise with envy. Butterflies flapped like damp handkerchiefs in the shimmering heat of the afternoon. Even the earthbound ants grew wings and flew. IT WAS UNFAIR.

Dragonflies rattled and reversed over pools, and damselflies, bright turquoise hyphens, hovered among the bulrushes.

Bats flew and fished the evening skies, airy mice on shivering parchment wings. Even seeds from brainless, thoughtless rooted plants were lifted into aimless flight on the slightest breeze. Every flying thing conspired to make the tortoise angry, unfairly treated by nature, so wingless, so solid, so very keen to leave the ground.

He wanted just for once to look down on the earth and to enjoy the vast freedom of the high thin air where the eagle circled, master of the sky. So it was to the eagle that the tortoise went. He asked the eagle ever so politely for lessons in the glorious art of flying. The eagle did not laugh at this.

"When you grow wings, my little pebble," he said. "You are as solid as the earth you walk upon." But the tortoise still insisted he was born to fly.
"Close cousin of a rock," said the eagle, "you are as airworthy as a stone." And he added not unkindly, "You are a tortoise and therefore aerodynamically suited to a slow life on the ground."
The tortoise was not deterred. "All I need is a little help. Once I'm free of the earth I can flap my legs."

After months of relentless pestering the tortoise, so thoroughly convinced of his flying ability and so desperate for a chance, touched the eagle's heart. If determination could keep a creature airborne, this one might yet fly.

And so the eagle took the tortoise up into the high thin air where his dreams had always flown, and there the eagle launched him into the clear sky and left him to the whim of GRAVITY AND THE WIND...

ACCEPT YOUR LIMITATIONS

ELEVEN

fool's gold

IN WHICH
A FARMER **LOSES**
HIS GOLDEN GOOSE

THERE WAS ONCE A GOOSE

WHO LAID, by strange and unlucky chance,
ONE GOLDEN EGG EACH DAY. Her owner considered himself
very fortunate, as this curious quirk of nature had steadily
helped him to become a wealthy man. He no longer needed to
work. His life became one of ease and comfort, and each day his
faithful goose laid another golden egg.

He had everything he needed and nothing to think about but
what he might buy next. As his desires became ever more
extravagant, he suggested to his goose that she lay her golden
eggs a little faster. There always seemed to be more things he
wanted than he had money to buy. He became impatient.

"Goose," he asked tersely, "perhaps you could try laying another
egg each day. Two eggs would be nice!" But she was no more
capable of changing her habits than any other goose.
"Three eggs a day?" he continued. "Yes, three would be enough…
or four. Four is a nice even number, not too much to ask…

But five, five is a handful, yes, maybe a handful a day… although six is a more usual number… for eggs. Half a dozen golden eggs would make me so happy…" And so he became a greedy man. "Seven … maybe eight, or nine. Nine is such a lovely number… three times three, very lucky… but then ten is so much easier… two handfuls… good for making calculations…," he said, calculating in his busy mind, "or eleven… maybe not eleven, neither one thing nor another… twelve, now there's a thought. Twelve! A lovely round dozen golden eggs each day… or a baker's dozen… thirteen, but thirteen is unlucky… add one more… fourteen, a handsome number but maybe not quite as good as fifteen…

TWENTY… THIRTY… FIFTY…

no, not good enough!"

He could not wait. He did not want to be counting eggs forever. No, he wanted every golden egg he was due NOW. No more waiting for the goose to lay, no more waiting to buy what he wanted to buy. It would be so much better to get all this out of the way so he could enjoy a life of ease, spending more and thinking less.

So he killed the goose for her golden eggs. But inside there was no hoard of treasure, no instant fortune, not even one single small golden egg more. With no goose there would be nothing… everyday… forever… nothing but hard work and sour regret.

THOSE WHO WANT EVERYTHING
MAY END UP WITH NOTHING

TWELVE

hArd cheese

IN WHICH A FOX PERSUADES
A CROW OUT OF HIS LUNCH

THERE WAS ONCE A CROW

sitting in a tree, holding a large, fresh cheese in his beak and feeling very pleased with himself. In fact, he was so pleased that he was just sitting there on his branch enjoying the all-round sense of well-being and smugness that the cheese was giving him WHEN A FOX WANDERED INTO THE STORY...

... A story that had begun when a freshly made cheese was left too close to an open window and the crow had stolen it. And would end, thought the fox confidently, with the cheese safely in his mouth. Another opportunity for trickery, thought the fox (and lunch)!

So the fox sat under the tree and looked up at the crow until at last the crow looked uneasily down at the fox.

"I was just admiring your particularly fine feathers," said the fox. "Have you discovered some new birdbath on your travels? Your eyes seem particularly bright too, and as for your toes... so dark and shiny... and your beak gleaming in the sunlight...

so perfectly set off by the creamy whiteness of whatever that is you have a hold of. Quite magnificent!" The crow was becoming more astonished and pleased with himself by the moment.

"And," continued the fox, "a little bird was saying only this morning that you're not just a pretty face. I was told that you can sing beautifully too. In fact, I understand you have the most remarkable singing voice for miles around... that you can move your audience from tears to laughter with a single note... that the nightingales hereabouts have all retired early..." Here the fox thought he had better stop, only adding, "How I would love to hear that melifluous voice of yours. It would be such a privilege. A private performance — a mere verse or two?..."

THE CROW, SO OVERWHELMED WITH FLATTERY, felt a helpless urge to sing.

He opened his beak...
        "CAW... CAW!" he went, unsweetly and tunelessly as only a crow can.

At the first note the cheese fell, bouncing from branch to branch to plummet into the fox's wide open, waiting jaws. And that's where the story, as the fox predicted, ends.

᪥ BEWARE OF FALSE FLATTERY ᪥

helen war

THERE WAS ONCE A LITTLE GIRL

WHO LIKED TO DRAW AND PAINT and make things, sometimes out of paper or fabric and sometimes out of mud, sticks and grass-clippings. She climbed trees and never fell out. She read lots of books and listened to what everyone told her, but she did not say much because she was very shy.

She wanted to be an illustrator and her parents, who were (and still are) artists, thought that this was a good idea. So, in a September gale, she went to the seaside where there was an art college to learn all about it. After three years she left and started to illustrate books for children. She had learned a little bit about her job but she kept learning and she thinks, if she keeps trying, that one day she might know enough to be good at it.

SHE LIKES WRITING STORIES TOO, but is very worried that one day somebody is going to make her sit down and take an exam in being a writer and then she will be found out.

She likes walking and watching the countryside and, when she has time, gardening and making things (though now not usually out of mud). What she likes most of all is her job and the people she works with.

She is less little now and she tries to be less shy. She is still wondering when or if she's supposed to grow up and, finally, she knows where there are some trees that need to be climbed...

TEMPLAR BOOKS
WRITTEN & ILLUSTRATED
BY HELEN WARD

the animals' christmas carol
1-84011-044-9

the cockerel and the fox
1-84011-515-7

the hare and the tortoise
1-84011-085-6

Just so stories
1-84011-315-4

the king of the birds
1-898784-63-9

old shell, new shell
1-84011-027-9

the wind in the willows
1-84011-019-8

TEMPLAR BOOKS WRITTEN
BY HELEN WARD

the boat
1-84011-402-9

the tin forest
1-84011-311-1

the dragon machine
1-84011-599-8

twenty-five december lane
1-84011-513-0

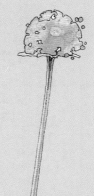

THE END

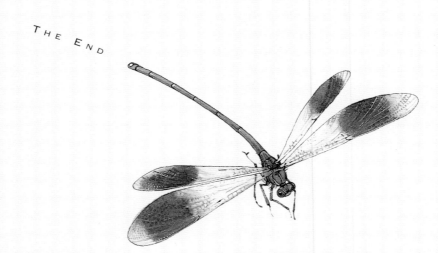

those who want everything
may end up with nothing

FINE FEATHER

DO NOT MAK

IT HOLDS THROUGH THE WHOLE SCALE OF CREATION THA

SLOW AND STEADY WINS THE RACE

DO NOT PUT OFF UNTIL TOMO

WHAT YOU